AUTO-B-GOOD

QUEEN FOR A DAY

A LESSON IN FAIRNESS

WRITTEN BY PHILLIP WALTON

ART BY RISING STAR STUDIOS

Free Activities, Coloring Pages, and Character Building Lessons Available Online!
www.risingstareducation.com

RISINGSTAR
S T U D I O S

QUEEN FOR A DAY: A Lesson in Fairness

Written by Phillip Walton

A story based on the characters from the series Auto-B-Good™

ART & EDITORIAL DIRECTOR
Tom Oswald

CONTRIBUTING EDITOR
Nick Rogosienski

ADDITIONAL EDITING
Colleen Sexton

LEAD 3D ARTIST
Phillip Walton

ADDITIONAL ART
Drew Blom
Bruce Pukema

GRAPHIC DESIGNER AND LETTERER
Steve Plummer

COVER DESIGN
Steve Plummer

PRODUCTION MANAGER
Nick Rogosienski

PRODUCTION COORDINATOR
Mark Nordling

SPECIAL THANKS
John Richards
Linda Bettes
Barbara Gruener
Jack Currier

Printed in China:
Shenzhen Donnelley Printing Co., Ltd
Shenzhen, Guangdong Province, China
Completed: February 2010
P1_0210

Publisher's Cataloging-In-Publication Data
(Prepared by The Donohue Group, Inc.)

Walton, Phillip.
  Queen for a day : a lesson in fairness / written by Phillip Walton ; art by Rising Star Studios.

    p. : ill. (holographic) ; cm. -- (Auto-B-Good)

  Previously published in 2009.
  Summary: A story based on the characters from the video series Auto-B-Good. As a part of Professor's fairness experiment, Cali gets to be 'queen for a day' and spends her time being unfair to her new servant, Izzi.
  Interest age level: 005-009.
  ISBN: 978-1-936086-44-3 (hardcover/library binding)
  ISBN: 978-1-936086-50-4 (pbk.)

1. Fairness--Juvenile fiction. 2. Role playing--Juvenile fiction. 3. Fairness--Fiction. 4. Kings, queens, rulers, etc.--Fiction. I. Rising Star Studios. II. Title.

PZ7.W3586 Qu 2010
[E]   2009913120

Bright and early one day, Izzi and Cali pulled into Professor's lab. "Good morning!" Professor said. "Thank you for helping me with my research into the reciprocal power dynamic of subservient relationships."

1

"What does that mean, Professor?" Izzi asked.

"Oh," Professor laughed. "It's a fairness experiment. It's a two-part test to see how fair both of you really are."

"Sounds exciting, Professor," Cali replied.

Professor smiled. "I call this test *'Queen for a Day.'*"

"Really?" Cali's eyes popped open.

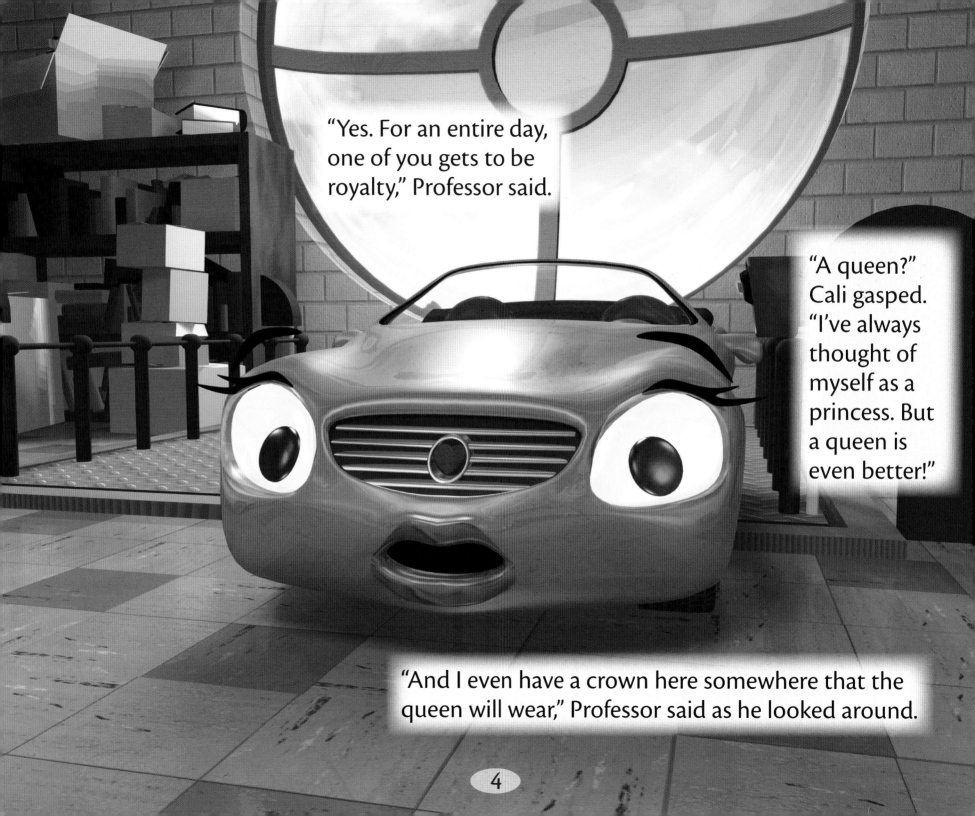

"Yes. For an entire day, one of you gets to be royalty," Professor said.

"A queen?" Cali gasped. "I've always thought of myself as a princess. But a queen is even better!"

"And I even have a crown here somewhere that the queen will wear," Professor said as he looked around.

"You mean this one?" Cali asked, suddenly wearing Professor's crown. "Does this mean I'm the queen?"

"Well, you should both agree that it's fair before we start the test. To be fair, you need to follow the rules and take turns. And don't take advantage of others either. Are you both sure that it's OK for Cali to be the queen?"

Izzi nodded. "It's all right, Professor. But I have a question. If Cali is the princess—"

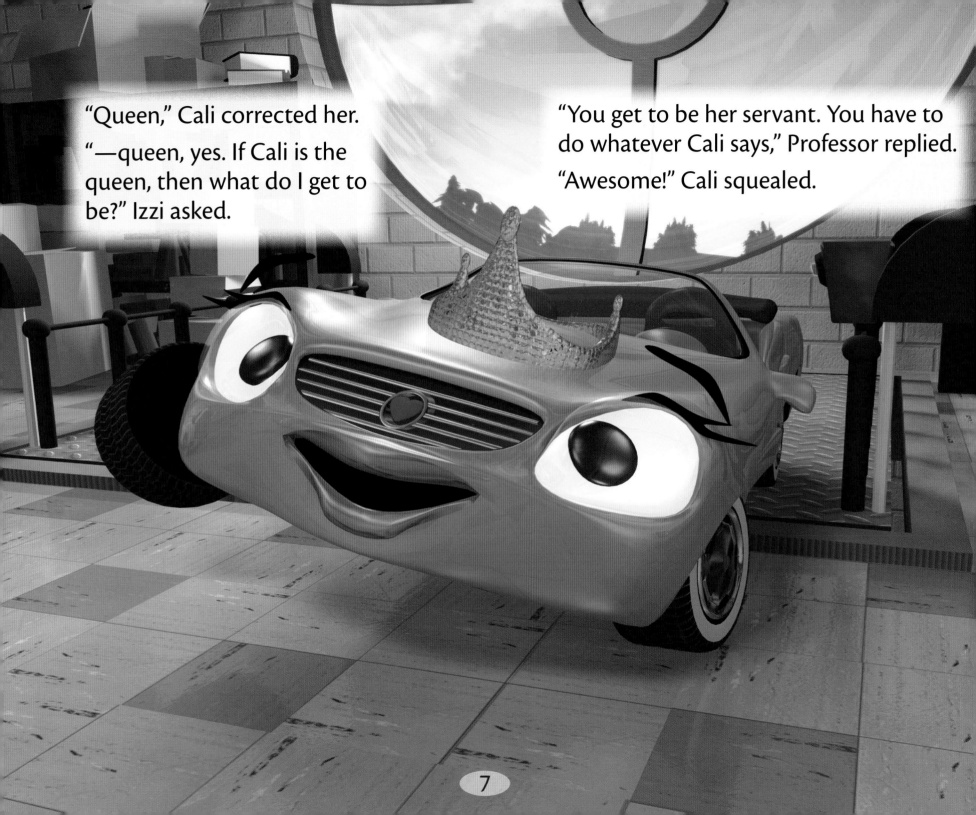

"Queen," Cali corrected her.
"—queen, yes. If Cali is the queen, then what do I get to be?" Izzi asked.

"You get to be her servant. You have to do whatever Cali says," Professor replied.
"Awesome!" Cali squealed.

"Don't worry, Professor," Cali smiled. "I should have no trouble being queen."

"Now, Cali, Izzi is your servant. But remember, you should still treat her fairly," Professor said.

9

"Just call me Queen Cali the Fair!" Cali replied. "Now let's go, Servant Izzi."

"Come back the same time tomorrow and we'll see how the test went," Professor said.

"Well, Servant Izzi? What do I want to do first?" Cali asked.

"We could go to the library," Izzi suggested.

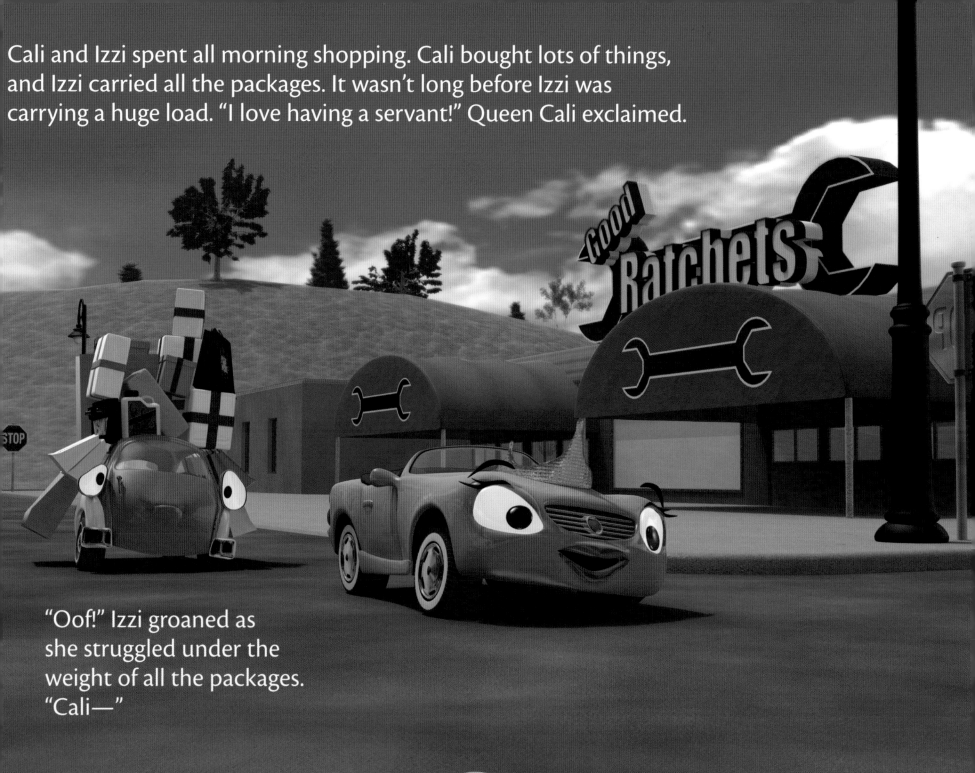

Cali and Izzi spent all morning shopping. Cali bought lots of things, and Izzi carried all the packages. It wasn't long before Izzi was carrying a huge load. "I love having a servant!" Queen Cali exclaimed.

"Oof!" Izzi groaned as she struggled under the weight of all the packages. "Cali—"

"Queen Cali, if you please," Cali grinned.

"Queen Cali… these packages are heavy. Could you carry something?" Izzi asked.

"Oh, if I must. It's only fair," Cali said. She pulled a new crown from the stack and put it on. "There!" she said. "Now we're both carrying stuff."

"But that's not—" Izzi started to say.

But Cali interrupted. "Tut, tut," she scolded. "Don't talk back to the queen. Now what should I do next?"

Izzi tried to answer, but Cali blurted out another idea. "I know! Squeekies!"

"I could use a wash too," Izzi said and wiped her sweaty brow.

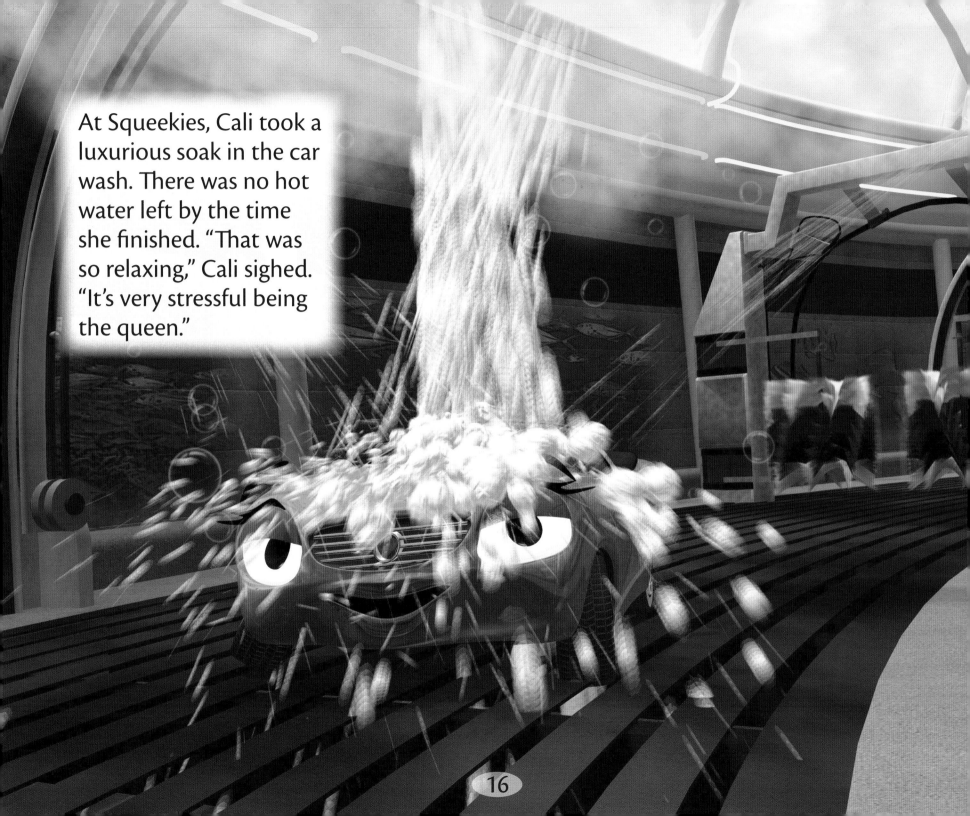

At Squeekies, Cali took a luxurious soak in the car wash. There was no hot water left by the time she finished. "That was so relaxing," Cali sighed. "It's very stressful being the queen."

Johnny was next in line at Squeekies. "Yeeoow!" he shrieked as he got a blast of icy water. He came out the other side shivering. "D-dude! Th-there's n-no h-hot w-w-water left," Johnny sputtered.

"I don't want to wash in cold water!" Izzi whined.

"Well, that's OK. We need to go anyway," said Cali. "I want to get a smoothie."

"But I'm still dirty," Izzi sighed.

18

"That's too bad, Servant Izzi," Cali said and drove off. Izzi struggled to keep up with her.

At the Rocky Road Ice-Cream Shop, Cali turned to Izzi. "I'm going inside for a smoothie," she said. "Servant Izzi, you wait here."

20

"But I'm thirsty too," Izzi said. "I'll just set your packages down and go with you."

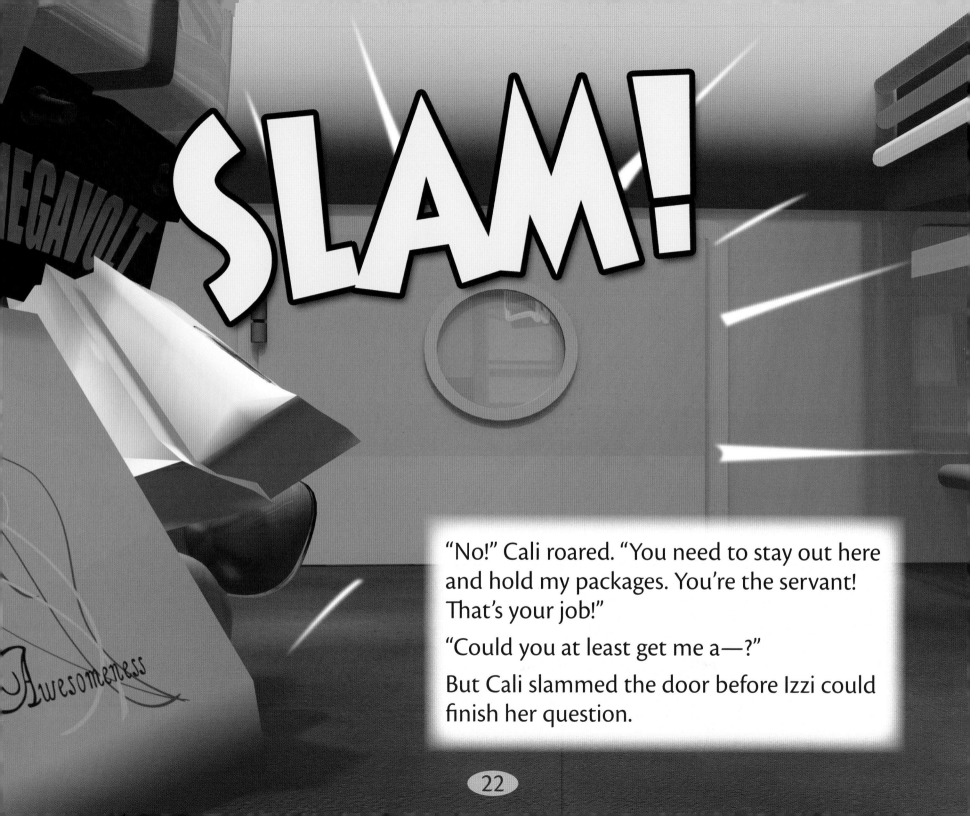

"No!" Cali roared. "You need to stay out here and hold my packages. You're the servant! That's your job!"

"Could you at least get me a—?"

But Cali slammed the door before Izzi could finish her question.

Izzi struggled to hold the heavy packages as the hot sun beat down on her. "This is silly. I shouldn't be treated this way. It's unfair," Izzi thought. She began to set down the packages.

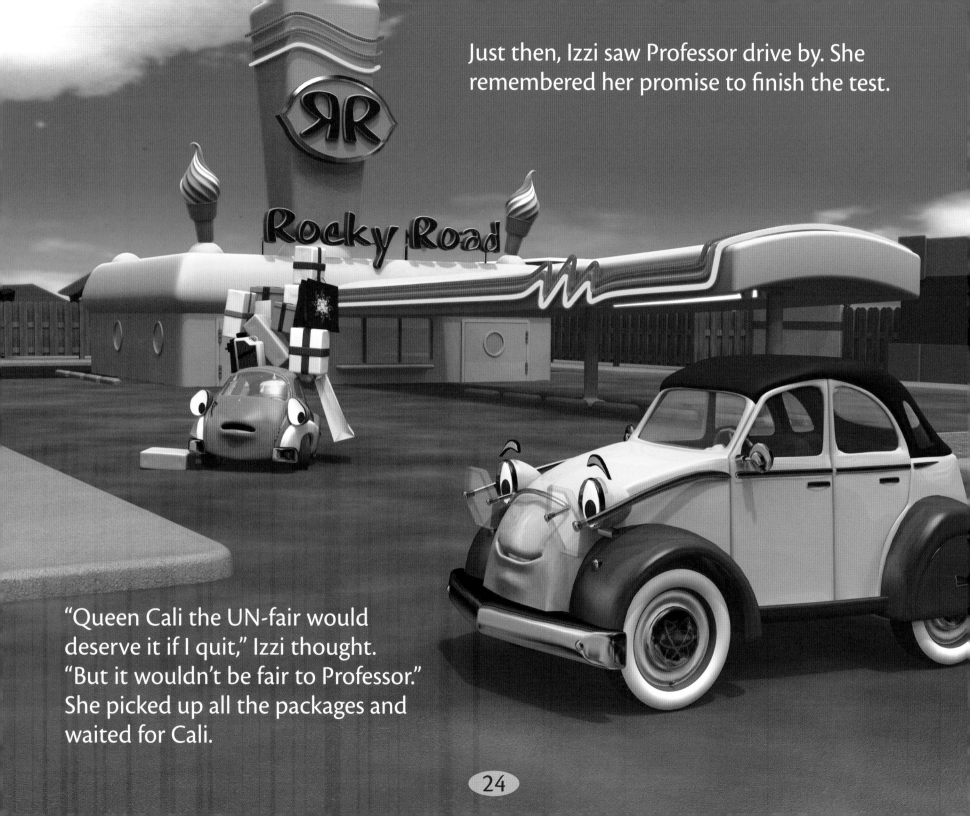

Just then, Izzi saw Professor drive by. She remembered her promise to finish the test.

"Queen Cali the UN-fair would deserve it if I quit," Izzi thought. "But it wouldn't be fair to Professor." She picked up all the packages and waited for Cali.

Cali finally exited
the Rocky Road
some time later.
"Well, let's get
all my new stuff
home!" she said.

25

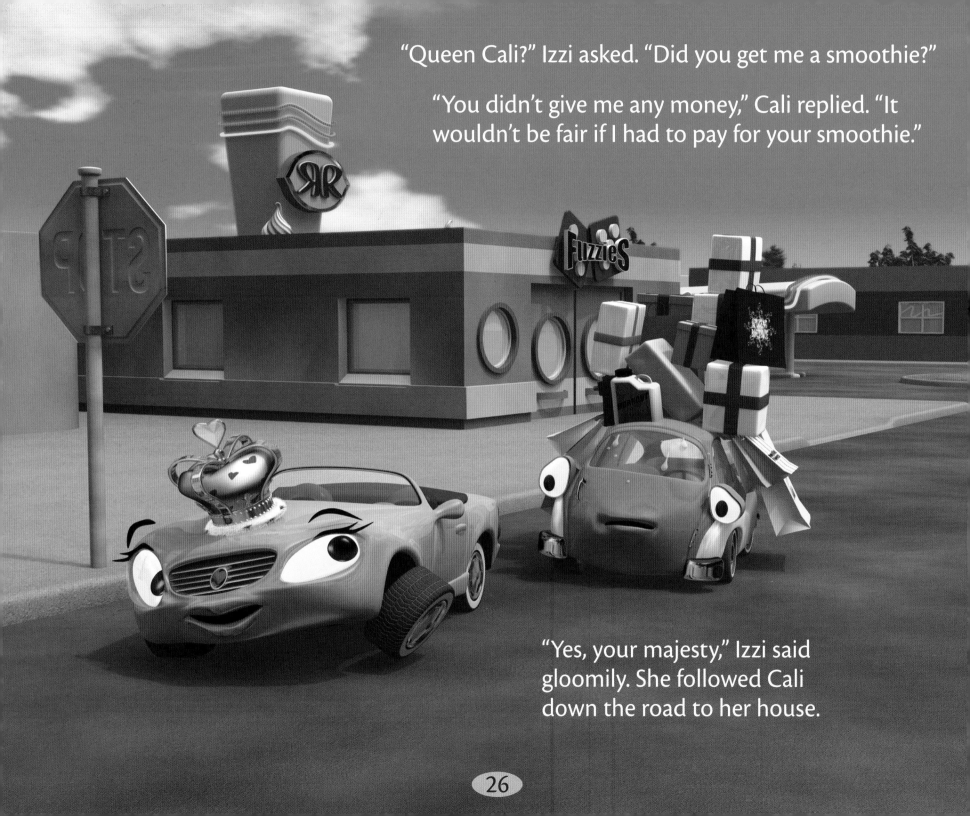

"Queen Cali?" Izzi asked. "Did you get me a smoothie?"

"You didn't give me any money," Cali replied. "It wouldn't be fair if I had to pay for your smoothie."

"Yes, your majesty," Izzi said gloomily. She followed Cali down the road to her house.

Izzi dropped off all of Cali's packages and turned to leave. "Servant? Where are you going?" Cali asked.

"I need to go home. I'm tired, and I have homework," Izzi moaned.

"Professor said I am queen for a day. You can't quit. It's not fair. You want to be fair, don't you?" Cali demanded.

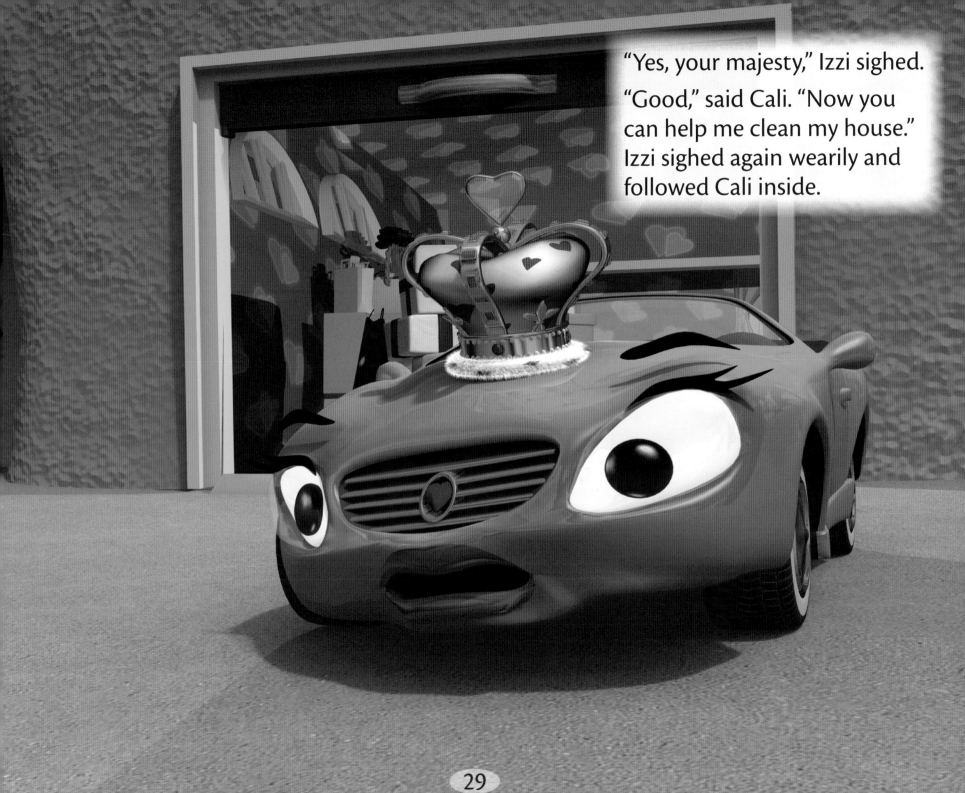

"Yes, your majesty," Izzi sighed.

"Good," said Cali. "Now you can help me clean my house." Izzi sighed again wearily and followed Cali inside.

Cali woke the next morning and put on her large crown. "It's good to be the queen," she said happily. "Now where is my servant?" Cali looked around. Izzi wasn't there.

"Servant!" she yelled. "Servant!" But there was no reply. "Oh...this is totally unfair!" Cali shrieked. "I'm the queen and my servant is gone. Professor is going to hear about this!"

Cali raced to Professor's lab. She was frazzled and out of breath. "Professor!" she yelled.

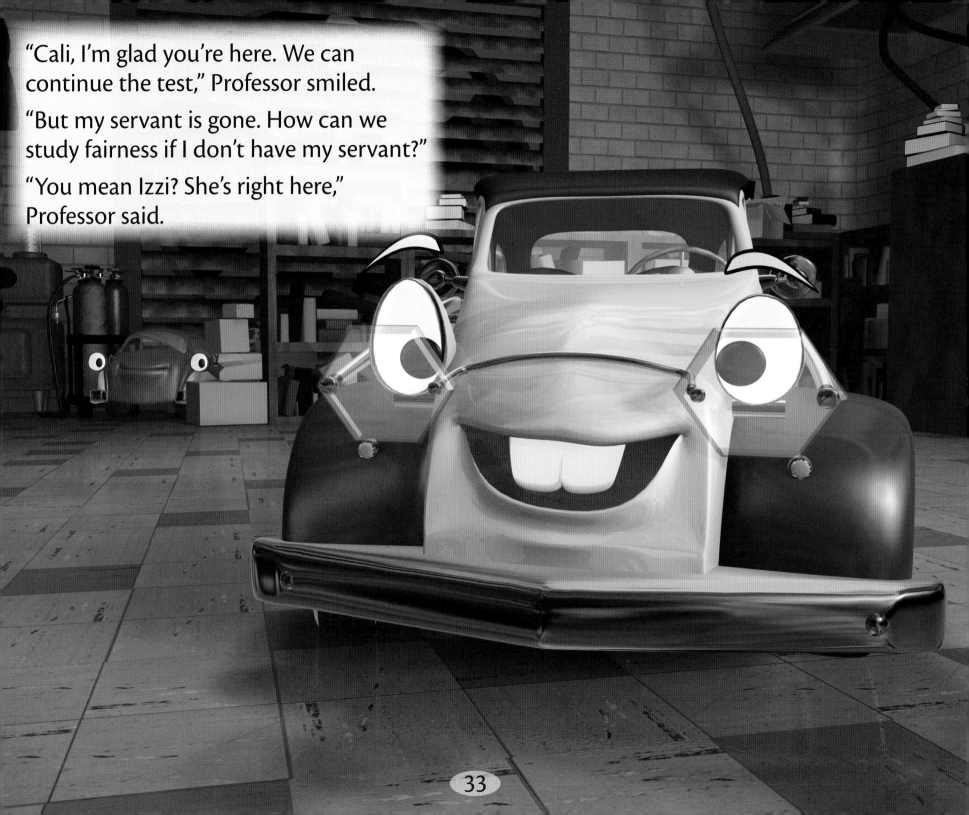

"Cali, I'm glad you're here. We can continue the test," Professor smiled.

"But my servant is gone. How can we study fairness if I don't have my servant?"

"You mean Izzi? She's right here," Professor said.

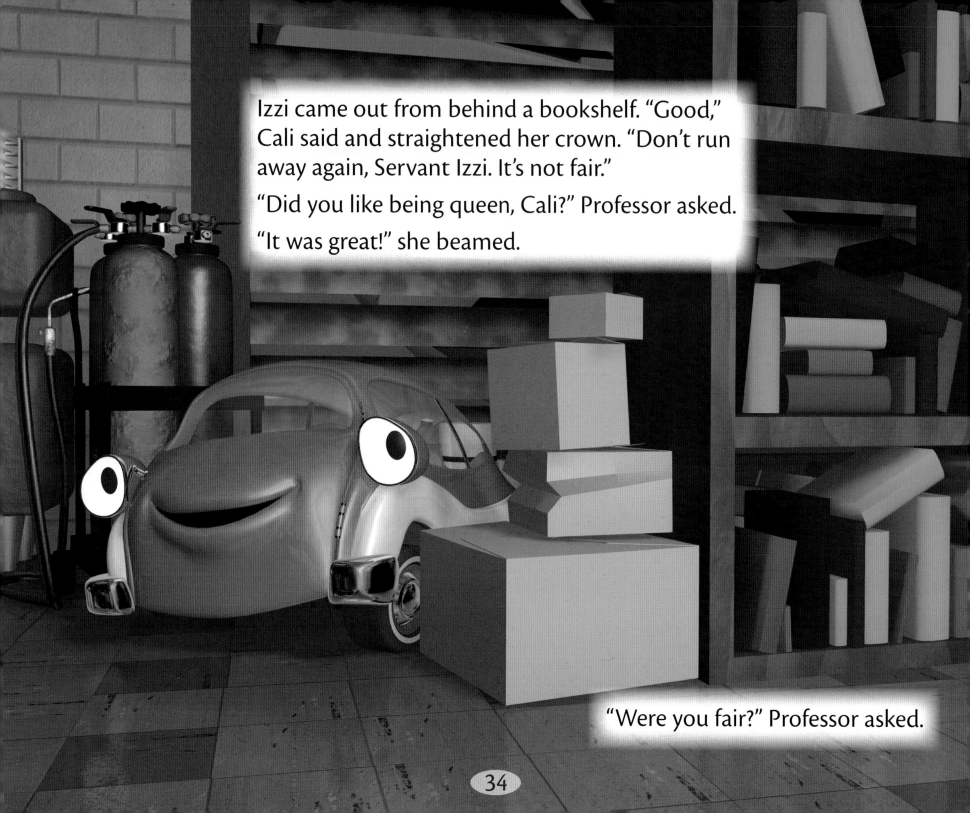

Izzi came out from behind a bookshelf. "Good," Cali said and straightened her crown. "Don't run away again, Servant Izzi. It's not fair."

"Did you like being queen, Cali?" Professor asked.

"It was great!" she beamed.

"Were you fair?" Professor asked.

"Of course," Cali said. But she wasn't quite sure. "I mean, I guess so."

"Izzi, did Cali treat you fairly?" asked Professor.

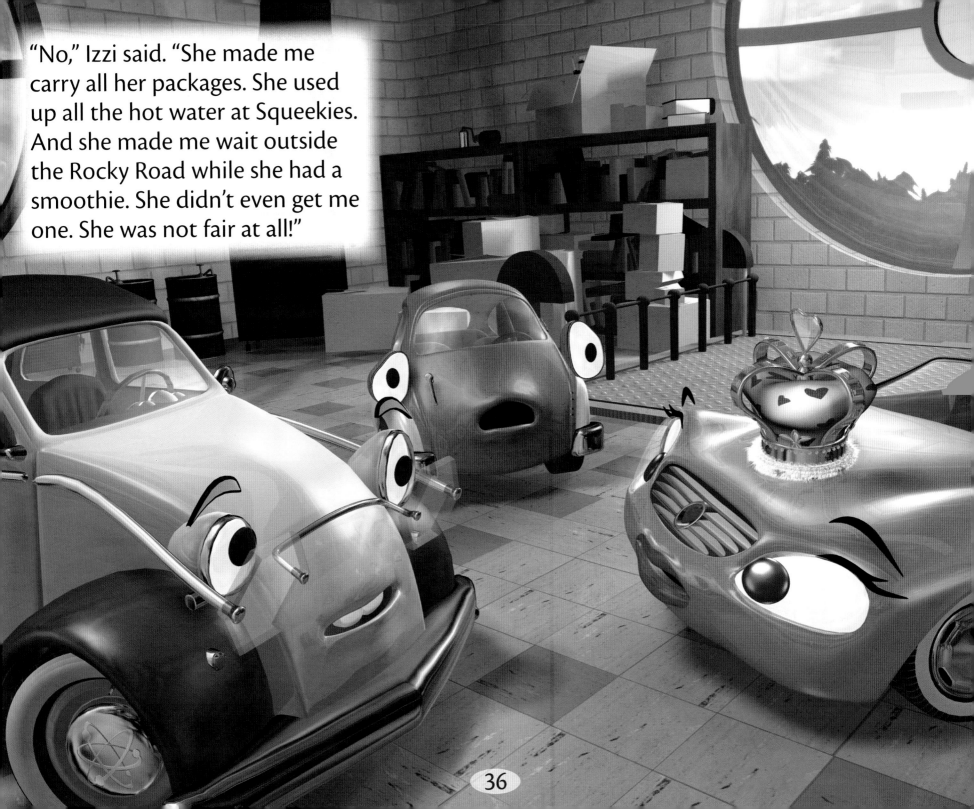

"No," Izzi said. "She made me carry all her packages. She used up all the hot water at Squeekies. And she made me wait outside the Rocky Road while she had a smoothie. She didn't even get me one. She was not fair at all!"

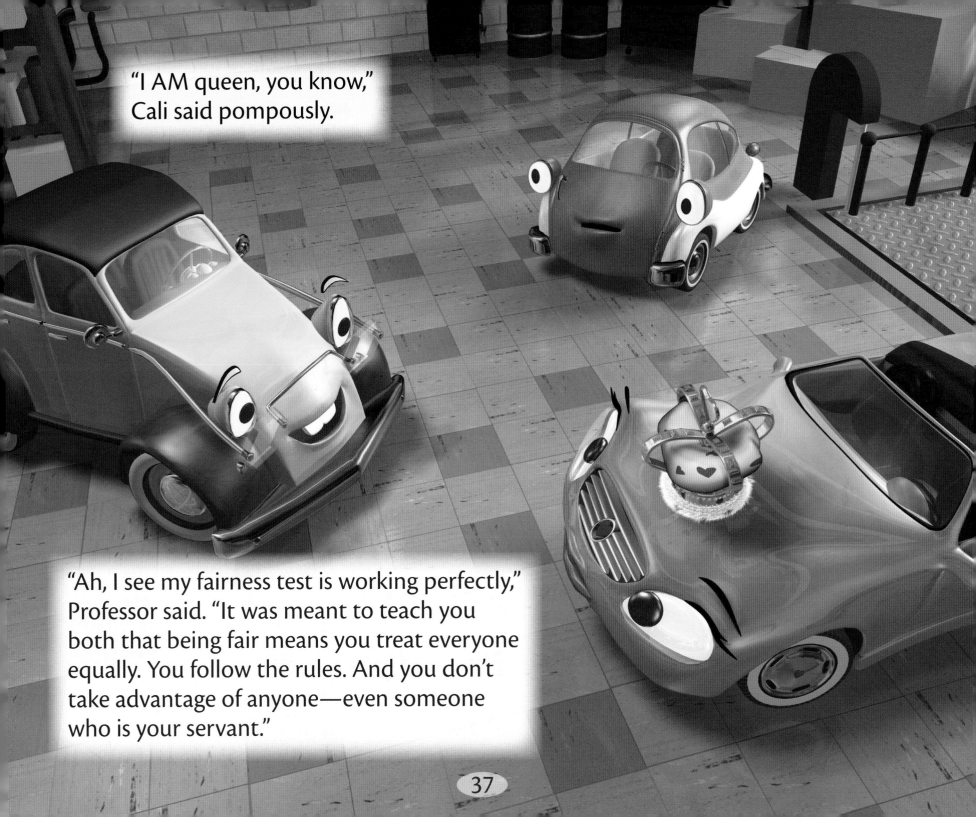

"I AM queen, you know," Cali said pompously.

"Ah, I see my fairness test is working perfectly," Professor said. "It was meant to teach you both that being fair means you treat everyone equally. You follow the rules. And you don't take advantage of anyone—even someone who is your servant."

"Well... I guess I was pretty unfair," Cali said. "I'm sorry, Izzi."

"From now on, it's fairness all the way."

"Well, Cali, in the second part of the test, Izzi gets to be Queen for a Day. And you will be <u>her</u> servant," Professor said.

Izzi smiled as she put on Professor's crown. "Oh," Cali said unhappily.

"Izzi, are you going to treat me the way I treated you?" Cali asked.

"I could…" Izzi said thoughtfully. "But that's not how I would want to be treated."

"Phew!" Cali sighed. "I thank you, Queen Izzi the Fair."

43

"Wonderful," Professor said. "You've both learned an important lesson. I think you'll very likely pass the fairness test!"